DISCARD

DISCARD

I am an ARO PUBLISHING THIRTY WORD BOOK
My thirty words are:

a	inbetween	should
brush (brushing)	it (it's)	sit
chair	like	spit
clean	machine	teeth
comes	my	there
Dentist's	pick	tiny
good	quick	to
gums	scratches	toy
he	see	wash
I (I'm)	shines	with

MY FIRST THIRTY WORD BOOKS

My First
Dentist Visit

Story by Julia Allen
Pictures by Bob Reese

 ARO PUBLISHING

See there.

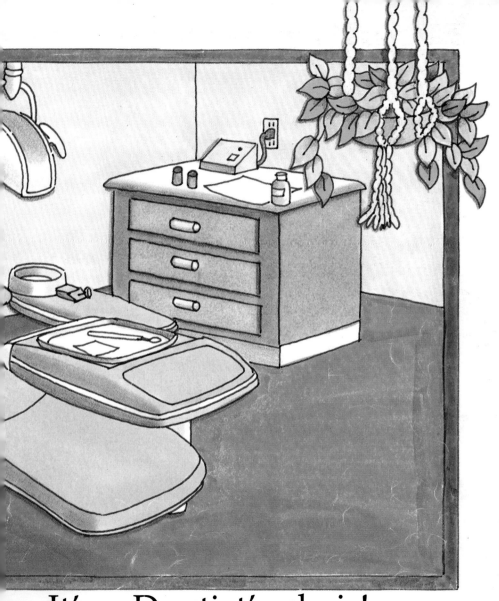

It's a Dentist's chair!

I'm good.

I sit like I should.

He comes

to see my gums.

9

I see a tiny pick.

He scratches with it quick.

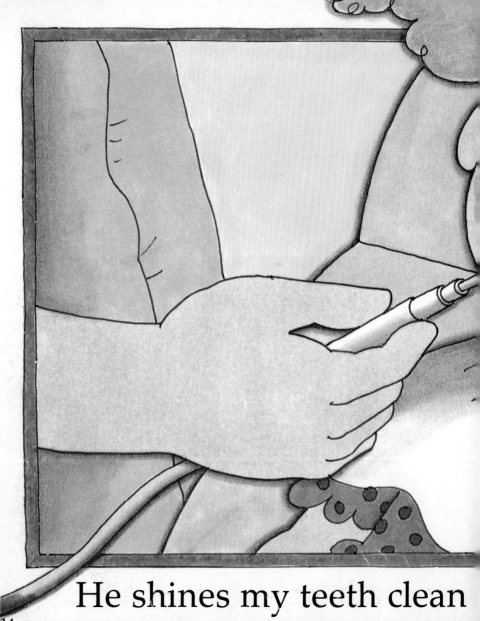

He shines my teeth clean

with a brushing machine.

It's good

to sit,

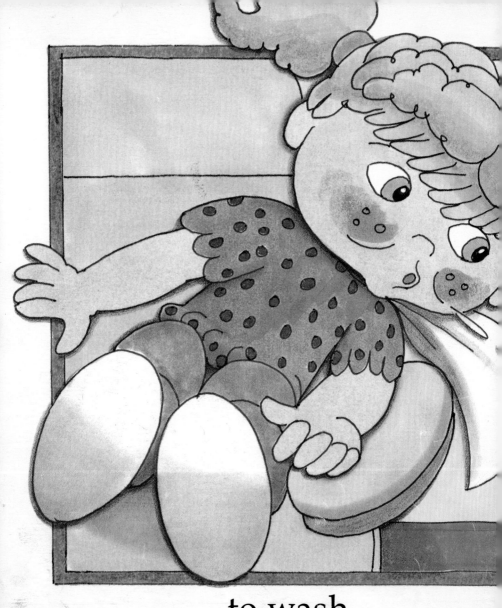

to wash,

to spit.

I like my teeth clean

inbetween.

I like to pick

a tiny toy quick!